PUFFIN BOOKS

THE FLYING SAVE!

Harry and the Dinosaurs

The Flying Save!

Ian Whybrow

Illustrated by Pedro Penizzotto

PUFFIN

PUFFIN BOOKS

Published by the Penguin Group
Penguin Books Ltd, 80 Strand, London WC2R 0RL, England
Penguin Group (USA) Inc., 375 Hudson Street, New York, New York 10014, USA
Penguin Group (Canada), 90 Eglinton Avenue East, Suite 700, Toronto, Ontario, Canada M4P 2Y3
(a division of Pearson Penguin Canada Inc.)
Penguin Ireland, 25 St Stephen's Green, Dublin 2, Ireland (a division of Penguin Books Ltd)
Penguin Group (Australia), 250 Camberwell Road, Camberwell, Victoria 3124, Australia
(a division of Pearson Australia Group Pty Ltd)
Penguin Books India Pvt Ltd, 11 Community Centre, Panchsheel Park, New Delhi – 110 017, India
Penguin Group (NZ), 67 Apollo Drive, Rosedale, Auckland 0632, New Zealand
(a division of Pearson New Zealand Ltd)
Penguin Books (South Africa) (Pty) Ltd, 24 Sturdee Avenue, Rosebank, Johannesburg 2196, South Africa

Penguin Books Ltd, Registered Offices: 80 Strand, London WC2R 0RL, England

puffinbooks.com

First published 2011
005

Text copyright © Ian Whybrow, 2011
Cover illustration copyright © Adrian Reynolds, 2011
Text illustrations copyright © Puffin Books, 2011
Character concept copyright © Ian Whybrow and Adrian Reynolds, 2011
All rights reserved

The moral right of the author and illustrators has been asserted

Set in Baskerville
Printed in Great Britain by Clays Ltd, St Ives plc

British Library Cataloguing in Publication Data
A CIP catalogue record for this book is available from the British Library

ISBN: 978–0–141–33281–9

www.greenpenguin.co.uk

MIX
Paper from
responsible sources
FSC
www.fsc.org   FSC® C018179

Penguin Books is committed to a sustainable
future for our business, our readers and our planet.
This book is made from Forest Stewardship
Council™ certified paper.

With grateful thanks to Anna, Thomas,

Laura and Sophie Campbell whose sense of fun

and combined spirit of adventure (including

dam-building down the Batch) inspired the

Grand Order of the Great Oak

Chapter 1

Harry was in trouble. A collection of special cards on his key-ring gave him command of the world's mightiest dinosaurs. Yet here he was, face-to-face with an evil little beast and with no back-up!

His room was a wreck. His most precious
things had been scattered everywhere. The
model plane he'd spent hours making had
been smashed to pieces. Now sharp teeth
were sinking into the palm of his hand, and
cruel green eyes stared up at him.

At least the screaming had stopped.

Harry gulped but tried not to make any sudden moves. He knew that to show fear could be a disaster.

The door handle turned and Mrs Brattburger came in, pushing the door open with her hip. She was carrying a tray loaded with drinks and cakes.

'Hey, you two! How are you getting along?' she called. 'Look what Harry's mummy has fixed for you!'

As Harry opened his mouth to say something, the wild-eyed monster unlocked its jaws. It was barely a metre high but moved sideways like a darting spider. It hurled itself at Mrs Brattburger and grappled her legs.

'Whoa!' cried Mrs Brattburger. She put the tray down on the bedside table. 'Feeding time!' she added cheerfully.

There was a gurgle from the pint-sized beast. 'Mum-mee! I don't like Harry!' it whined.

Harry looked at the tooth-marks on his hand. Mrs Brattburger looked at the general mess and made a sad face. Her little monster looked at both of them and began to sob loudly.

'There, there, Frederick darling!' she cooed, clasping him to her chest. She gave Harry a knowing look over the boy's head. 'Don't worry, Harry,' she said in a loud whisper. 'You wouldn't believe how *sensitive* he is. He has a real problem making friends. I guess it's just his age. But if you could just be patient with him, Mr Brattburger and I would be *so-o-o* grateful. It's a terrible problem finding a place to leave him while we're away on business. But then your mother offered. So kind of her!'

She cradled Frederick's red, screwed-up face in her hands and said to him, 'Harry really likes you, darling. You'll soon be getting along just fine, you'll see! When Daddy and I get back, you can tell us all about the *heaps* of fun you had together. Am I right, Harry?'

Yeah, right, thought Harry, rubbing his sore hand.

Chapter 2

'You were too soft on him,' said Siri. As the only child of two professors, he liked to give his opinions loud and clear. 'If some little kid wrecked my room I would soon show him who's the boss!'

'And he actually *bit* you?' said Charlie. 'Wow!' She turned up the lamp.

The shadowy faces of the Grand Order of the Great Oak members – the GOGOs for short – grew clearer. Harry had called an emergency meeting and they were squeezed up pretty tight in the belly of their secret oak-tree den. It was more of a squash than usual because Charlie had insisted on

cramming her precious skateboard in with her. She'd painted the dragon on it herself and it was her pride and joy.

'If he bit *me*,' Siri added, pushing up his glasses, 'I would have bitten him back!'

'What, even if he was only three and a half years old? Even if his mother was your mother's boss?' challenged Harry. 'His parents own one of the magazines my mother writes for. It's called *Parenting Without Pain*.'

'Tuh!' muttered Charlie. '*They're* parents and *Frederick's* a pain.'

'Everybody says he's got problems,' said Harry.

'That's weird,' said Jack. He liked action more than words, so he didn't usually say much. 'How come?'

'He's spoilt rotten,' said Charlie.

'So,' said Siri, 'these Brattburger people are very important. And this is why you all have to be nice to their son. Am I right?'

'Exactly,' said Harry. 'And he's staying for another two nights –'

Jack finished his sentence for him. '– while his mum and dad go to Scotland on business. Hmmm.'

'Sam won't have anything to do with

him,' Harry complained. 'She says I'm the boy of the family so it's up to me to keep him happy.'

'Don't worry about your sister!' cried Siri. 'We GOGOs stick together! I say that we all help Harry by trying to make friends with this kid. All those in favour?'

Harry looked around hopefully. Never in the history of the GOGOs had hands gone up so slowly.

Chapter 3

'It's really good of you to give Nan and
me a break,' said Mum as the GOGOs
gathered in the kitchen at Harry's house.
You could see from the look on her face
that she knew it wouldn't be easy for them
to keep Frederick happy. 'I've got to finish
some work before lunchtime and Nan has
to bake cakes for her gardening club. We've
already had to change his clothes twice
this morning, so do try to keep him clean
as well as happy.' She leaned down and set

Frederick's sunhat straight. 'You're a lucky boy having all these big children to play with,' she said in an extra-cheery voice. 'So you be good and hold their hands.'

'Bum-bum!' said Frederick and threw down the hat.

Harry would have been marched up to his room if he'd behaved like that. And

he could tell Nan was definitely thinking
about it. She flumped a spoonful of butter
into her bowl so hard that a cloud of flour
flew into the air.

'Who wants a go on my skateboard?'
asked Charlie, stepping forward quickly. 'It's
a special one called Dragon.'

Mum and Nan looked at each other and
crossed their fingers as the GOGOs fixed
smiles on their faces and led Frederick out
of the back door.

Charlie put the board down on the
grass and hopped on. Frederick ran at her
and tried to push her off it. 'Hey! Steady,
Freddie!' she said. 'Wait till I show you how
to stand on it.'

'NOT Freddie! My name is Fred-er-

RICK. Call me Frederick J. Brattburger!'
he shouted, still pushing at Charlie. Without
pausing for breath, he gritted his teeth and
added, 'I know how to do skateboards. Get
off!'

Charlie thought about telling him that
her name was Charlotte Squirt-Squeezer

but changed her mind. She stepped off her pride and joy and watched while Frederick began to kick it and stamp on it. 'You do it like this!' he declared. 'You make it jump up.' He knocked Dragon sideways and scraped his shoe over it a couple of times.

'Yes, well . . . how about scooting on it first, just to get your balance?' suggested Charlie, trying to show him how. She was getting worried about the paintwork.

'NO! NOT LIKE THAT!' yelled Frederick, shoving her away. He carried on kicking at it. When the board didn't do what he wanted, he picked it up and held it to his chest.

'So much for skateboarding,' muttered Harry. He raised his voice, put on a big smile and said, 'OK, who's for a bounce on the trampoline?'

'Wait!' said Siri. 'It's a warm day. Let's teach Frederick water-bombing.' He reached into his pocket and pulled out a bunch of mini balloons. 'Here we go, everybody.

Help yourselves.' All the GOGOs grabbed a handful.

Frederick clung grimly to the skateboard and staggered after them, watching carefully in silence as they filled a balloon each at the garden tap and tied off the necks.

'Garage door! Nearest to the handle wins!' cried Siri. The GOGOs lined up and took it in turns to throw a balloon from where they were standing. Charlie was last to throw.

SPLAT! Bang on target!

'Great shot!' everyone yelled.

'Your turn now. I filled this for you,' said Siri, holding out a bulging red water-bomb to Frederick. 'Take one of these and see if you can hit the garage door with it. You can go closer if you like.'

Frederick was in such a hurry to get hold of the balloon that he forgot he was holding the skateboard and smacked Siri round the ear with it.

'OUCH!' wailed Siri, falling on his back and then, 'SPLAGHHH!' as Frederick whacked the water-bomb in his face.

'Gimme another one!' shouted Frederick, squealing with delight.

The rest of the GOGOs decided to play safe and hastily tucked their unfilled balloons into their pockets.

Frederick was furious. He snatched back Charlie's dragon-board. 'I hate you all!' he announced. 'I'm going to tell Harry's mummy.' He started to head for the back door.

'Oh no!' muttered Harry, and then he called, 'Who wants to go on the trampoline?'

'Me!' chorused the GOGOs. 'Come on, Frederick!' They dashed over to the other side of the garden. 'Let's have some FUN.'

Nimbly, Jack clambered up the ladder on

to the trampoline.

He did a few warm-up

bounces, then a back-flip.

'Look at that!' said Siri.

His voice was full of admiration

as he wiped his glasses clear with one

hand and rubbed his sore ear with

the other. 'Jack's in the school team.

He can teach you some *excellent*

moves, Frederick.'

Jack lay flat and looked over the edge
of the trampoline. 'Come up and try it,
Frederick,' he said, reaching down. 'Give him a
leg-up, Siri.'

'NO! ME DO IT!' screamed Frederick.
He threw himself at the ladder and quickly
discovered that he couldn't climb up and hang
on to the dragon-board at the same time.

He tried again. He fell off. He dropped
the skateboard with a clatter on to his foot.
The corners of his
mouth turned down.
He opened his mouth
and started to howl.
'YOU MADE ME
HURT MYSELF!
WAAAAAAH!'

Chapter 4

After Nan had looked at Frederick's foot
and stopped him crying for the third time
in as many hours, she suggested a walk.
'You need to wear him out,' she said to the
GOGOs. 'Use up some of his energy – then
maybe he'll have a little nap this afternoon.'

'Some hopes,' said Harry.

'Best not to get him over-excited,' she
said quietly into Harry's ear. 'There's plenty
of hazelnuts about. Take him down the
Batch to pick some. That'll do it.' Then she

spoke loud enough for Frederick to hear.
'Let Freddie carry the bag to collect the
nuts in. You'll like that, won't you, Freddie?'

'I want a bucket, not a bag,' announced
Frederick.

'Oh dear, you are a fusspot,' said Nan.
'Ask Harry nicely and maybe he can find
you one.'

'And a spade,' said Frederick. 'I only like
a bucket *with* a spade.' Nan gave him one of
her special looks. 'Please,' he added quickly.

Well, please is a start, Harry thought. Nan
watched him unhook the attic trapdoor
while the GOGOs kept an eye on Freddie.

The aluminium ladder clicked as it
dropped down, and Harry climbed up
through the hatch.

'Hold on tight, Harry,' called Nan. 'Be careful.'

Harry crawled into the attic and felt for the light switch. Then he walked carefully over the thick boards that were lying across the beams.

The attic was crammed with lots of boxes filled with things like old toys and Christmas decorations. In the corner was the box Harry was looking

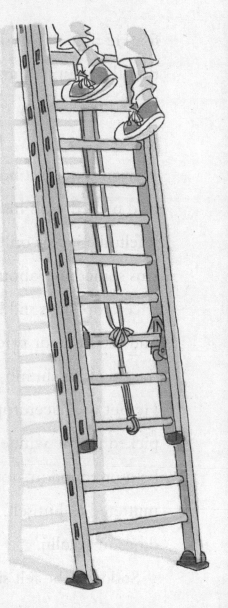

for. He tipped it upside down. The sound that the plastic dinosaurs made as they rattled softly on to the dusty planks gave him a start.

Even though it had been years since he'd played with his bucketful of dinosaurs, it felt like it was only yesterday. There was something about the way the little triceratops' legs slid between his fingers and the familiar prickle of its horns against the tip of his thumb that made him smile. He put the triceratops down carefully and picked up the winged lizard. 'You should be a pteranodon, not a pterodactyl,' he muttered to himself. 'And you're not even a dinosaur, really.'

Suddenly he felt silly. He was *way* too old

for games with toy dinosaurs and here he
was talking to them again! But he couldn't
stop himself tidying them up, as if it were
mean to let them just lie in a tangled heap.
He took the bucket out, found the spade
that went with it and then put all the
dinosaurs carefully back into the empty box.

He felt into his pocket for his key-ring
and pulled it out. A collection of cards in the
shape of dinosaurs was attached, and Harry
thought back to how he'd got them. Years
after he had put his bucketful of dinosaurs
away for good, he had been lying in bed
when – WHAM! – a full-size spinosaurus
had turned up. What a moment! Wow! Even
now he could hardly believe it.

Spinosaurus had given him the key-ring

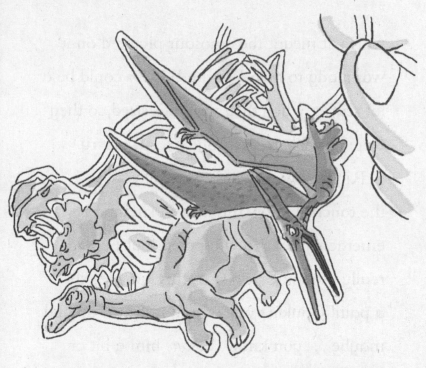

and explained that it gave Harry the power,
if ever he had a real emergency, to call up
any dinosaur to help him. Because he had
taken such good care of his toy dinosaurs
when he was younger, this was their way of
paying him back. They were his B.U.Ds –
Back-Up Dinosaurs – and when a card was

warm, it meant the dinosaur pictured on it was ready to help. But the B.U.Ds could be a lot scarier when they were life-sized, so they were invisible to everyone except Harry.

Right now the cards were all cool to the touch. 'I know this is not exactly an emergency,' Harry whispered, 'but I could really use some help with this kid. He's such a pain! Couldn't one of you just turn up and maybe . . . you know . . . *scare* him a bit or something?'

Nan's voice snapped him out of his daydream. 'Harry! Have you found that bucket and spade yet?'

'I've got them,' he answered, slipping the key-ring back into his pocket. 'I'm coming down.'

Chapter 5

'I hate rubber boots,' said Frederick.

'We all do,' Siri told him as he and Jack steered him down the lane towards the footpath that dropped down a bank into the woods everyone called the Batch. 'But it can get pretty muddy down here.'

'Gimme my spade!' ordered Frederick.

'No. You've got to hold hands with Jack and Siri in case a car comes down the lane,' explained Charlie as she tried her best to hide the dragon-board behind her back.

Fortunately, at the point where the path divided, Mr Oakley appeared with his big bouncy dog, Morgan. Mr Oakley owned the nearest farm up the lane from Harry's house and had been a friend of the family for as long as Harry could remember. Morgan didn't normally walk on a lead, and Mr Oakley had to give him a tug as he tried to race up to greet the children. Whimpering and yelping for joy, the dog huffed and wagged his tail about.

The GOGOs gave him a thunderous patting and a good scratch behind the ears. Strangely, Frederick stood still and was quiet.

'What's he on the lead for?' Harry asked after everyone had said hello.

'Big alert on,' said Mr Oakley, reaching over to make Morgan sit down. 'I just had a word with Johnny Booker from the Spansford estate. He told me all the workers just got orders to shoot any stray dogs they see wandering about. There's been another lot of sheep-worrying.'

'Do you mean the sheep were injured?' asked Charlie.

'Not bitten or nothing, no, but Johnny had to rescue a couple that got chased off estate land. They ran into that thorn hedge just up there, where I keep my young rams,' said Mr Oakley, pointing across the stream. 'They got panicked, see, and when that happens, they can struggle something terrible and lose their strength. And if you don't find 'em in time, they can drop dead of fright. I've lost sheep that way myself.'

'Morgan wouldn't chase sheep, though,' said Jack, squeezing the dear old dog's head under his arm.

'Wouldn't hurt a fly,' said Mr Oakley. 'But Colonel and Lady Spansford have given the order to destroy *any* loose dogs, and I don't want to take no chances. Especially since Her Ladyship has fallen out with me just at the moment. Which is a pity, because my young cows need a nice bit of fresh grass and I was hoping to rent one of her spare fields.'

'What happened?' asked Siri politely. The GOGOs couldn't imagine Mr Oakley falling out with anyone.

'Well, as you know,' explained the farmer, scratching his white beard, 'Colonel and Lady Spansford are quite soppy about their little terrier, Spike. He's a nice little dog, but they *will* let him go chasing off after the animals when they take him across the fields for a walk. They think it's funny. "Oh, he won't hurt them!" they say. "He's

only a tiny creature!" But what they don't understand is that he upsets 'em, see? He makes 'em run. And that's no good for a sheep with a lamb inside her. I told her Ladyship that she should keep him on the lead, so she's not too pleased with me.'

'Will *any* sort of dog attack a sheep?' asked Jack.

'Well, I tell you what,' said Mr Oakley.
'It only takes one dog to run a bit wild and
he'll go round gathering others. And then
they all get caught up in the excitement,
and they start what they call "packing"
– that means they gather in a pack like
wolves. That's when you've got to watch
out, because they're not nice tame pets any
more when they get like that.'

All this time, Frederick had quietly
been watching Morgan. Here at last was
something he was really interested in. He
lifted the plastic spade above his head and
stepped forward.

'Here! Don't you go clonking Morgan
with that, young man!' warned Mr Oakley.

But for once, Frederick wasn't being

violent. 'I throw it for him,' he said. But as
he raised it behind his head to do just that,
Morgan moved forward and gently took
the handle in his mouth and laid the spade
across the toes of the boy's rubber boots.
Frederick was thrilled.

'Good boy,' said Mr Oakley, though it wasn't clear whether he meant Frederick or Morgan. He gave all the children a nod of goodbye and walked away with Morgan towards the lane.

'You all go careful now,' he shouted behind him.

Chapter 6

Nutting was no fun at all. Frederick made a fuss because he couldn't understand where to look for nuts. He made a fuss because he couldn't reach them when they were pointed out. Then he made a fuss about them being put into his bucket. He moaned because the shells were too hard and they tasted horrible when he tried to crack them open. And when they were cracked for him, he moaned because the nuts made him cough.

'Never go nutting with a nutter,' murmured Siri with a sigh.

'I bags we take him home,' said Charlie.

'But we haven't really worn him out yet,' said Harry, remembering what Nan had said.

'Well, he's bound to enjoy making a dam,' suggested Jack.

'The only problem is . . . how are we going to keep him clean and dry?' Charlie wondered.

'Don't worry. I will speak to him,' said Siri. 'I shall tell him to use common sense.' He tucked his trousers into his wellies and waded into the stream. 'Look here, Frederick. You see how the water flows this way?' He dropped in a leaf and gave it time

to bob downstream. 'Well, we are going
to make a small wall of mud and turn the
water so that it makes a nice lake over
there. You can do the spade-work. But it is
very important to enter the water slowly
and carefully. That way you won't . . .'

It took Frederick three seconds to rush

forward, trip
over a stone,
do a belly-flop
into the shallow
water and stand
up screaming
his head off. 'I
HATE YOU
ALL! I WANT
MY MUMMY!'

'Now what do we do?' asked Harry.

The answer appeared out of the bushes behind them with a crash. Everyone whirled round and ducked down, waiting to see what had caused the noise.

It was a wild-eyed scraggy dog, with tangled and torn fur. Its long skinny body and legs were shaking, and a greyish tongue swung out of its mouth. As if it didn't look scary enough, then it barked.

'BWOOOOF! BWOOOOF!'

In a flash, everyone had the same thoughts. *This is the wild dog, the worrier, the sheep-killer!*

Then a voice said, 'Here, boy!' It was Frederick, muddy and dripping in the stream. 'Here, Shaky!'

'Um, no, Frederick,' Harry warned
quietly out of the corner of his mouth. 'Best
not to call the doggie. We'll all just stand
nice and quiet until he goes away, shall we?'

'Come on, boy!' Frederick called again.

With a yelp – or a snarl – the beast
hurled itself towards the child.

'Look out!' yelled the GOGOs.

Too late. The dog had covered the ground in a flash. It threw itself into the water. Frederick leaned forward and patted its shivering back.

The dog barked, then grabbed the boy's sleeve in its teeth. It whined and began to tug. Frederick giggled and allowed himself to be pulled out of the stream and on to dry land.

As soon as the boy was out of the water, the dog dashed along the path, woofing like thunder and bouncing up and down on its front legs. 'Coming!' called Frederick – and dashed after him.

The GOGOs looked at each other. 'Come on,' said Harry, and they all took off behind.

The dog kept ahead most of the way, inviting the children to follow with barks that made their ears ring. Sometimes he dashed sideways through the woods and came up behind them, grumbling and

snapping at their heels as if they were a flock of sheep. Shaky was the sheep-worrier, all right. Harry and his friends were certain of that.

Soon they were on the lane and then outside the gate of Harry's house. The dog ran a little further up the lane, stopped

and waited, trembling and whining and yawning in a nervous sort of way that showed its long yellow fangs. Frederick, looking equally wild and messy, ran after the dog and threw his arms around its neck.

'Um, I wouldn't do that, Frederick,' suggested Harry. 'I think the doggie needs to go home now.'

Frederick wasn't having any of that. 'No! He loves me!' he said.

'BWUFF! BWUFF! BWUFF!' answered the dog with its loud bark.

Charlie had an idea. 'He's saying he wants you to come upstairs and get changed out of your wet things,' she whispered. 'Quick!'

For the first time since he had arrived at

Harry's, Frederick did what he was told and went quietly with the GOGOs as they smuggled him into Harry's room and sorted out dry clothes for him to wear.

Shaky sat just as quietly at the front door until the GOGOs returned with Frederick, all of them creeping down the stairs. They'd just opened the front door without being spotted when Sam stepped into the hallway.

Harry's older sister was all dressed up to go shopping with her friend Melody. Her lips were shiny with red lip-gloss and she had her new denim jacket on. Suddenly she spotted Shaky on the doorstep, and Frederick with his arms wrapped around the dirty creature. 'Argh! Keep them away

from me!' she squealed.
'Look at the state of
that kid, Harry! What
will his parents say if
they see him like that?'

'Oh, blame me, why
don't you?' said Harry.

Her shouting sent
the dog backing away
from the door. Freddie

let go as Shaky scampered off, jumped
over the front gate and ran into the lane,
barking like mad.

Frederick ran after him. 'Shaky! Come
back!'

'Freddie, stop!' shouted Jack, racing after
the small boy.

As Frederick dashed blindly out of the gate, a tractor came rumbling round the bend in the lane.

At exactly that moment Mum and Nan
came rushing into the garden, alerted by
Sam yelling, 'Look out!'

Chapter 7

Jack hurled himself after Frederick and grabbed him, pushing him to safety on to the grass verge. The tractor driver shouted at them as he rumbled by.

'Come back, Shaky!' wailed Frederick. But the dog was so scared by the fuss and noise that he dived under the hedge on Mr Oakley's side of the lane and ran off across the field.

There was no calming Frederick after that. He bawled, he sobbed, he wanted his mummy, his daddy and his Shaky. Nothing else in the world would do.

Harry thought he would never hear the end of it. It was all his fault, according to Sam.

Mum and Nan weren't too pleased either. 'All we asked you to do was amuse him for a couple of hours!' they complained.

Harry escaped into the garden where Charlie, Siri and Jack were sitting glumly

on the grass with their chins in their hands.

'There's only one thing for it,' said Harry.
'We've got to find that dog.'

'How?' asked Siri. 'It obviously doesn't
come from around here. And you heard
what Mr Oakley said. All the farmers
around here know about the sheep-
worrying. If they see a stray dog they're

going to shoot it, not catch it.'

'All the more reason to find Shaky before they do, then!' said Harry.

'And what if he's innocent . . .?' asked Jack.

'He didn't *act* innocent,' said Charlie. 'He looked pretty savage to me.'

'But he didn't do us any harm,' said Jack. 'OK, he looks fierce and he's got a scary bark, that's all. You shouldn't judge animals by the way they look and sound, any more than people.'

'Exactly!' said Harry. 'It would be terrible if Shaky got shot and it turned out to be another dog that was after the sheep. And the other thing is – Frederick's crazy about that animal. He thinks it loves him. You all saw how much nicer he was with Shaky around.'

'You're right!' said Siri. 'We've got to find him.'

The GOGOs all nodded their heads and quickly agreed on a plan. They would split up and do a proper search of the area by bike . . . and skateboard, of course. First they would check out all the dogs in the village just in case Shaky went creeping round to invite them to join his pack.

'Meet down by the bakery in an hour,' said Charlie, strapping on her kneepads. 'GOGOs to the *dog*-rescue!'

Harry made sure his water bottle was firmly locked into its cage, turned left at

the junction and puffed off towards
Hanter Hill. His friends shot off
down towards the village, Siri on
his bike, Jack standing on the pedals
of his BMX and Charlie rumbling
along on Dragon.

Shaky looks as if he's a stray, Harry thought to himself. He had no collar and no one had seen him before. Harry had an idea: maybe he was a farm dog from one of the hill farms around the valley.

Tucked into his back pocket, wrung out but still damp, was Frederick's wet T-shirt. He thought Shaky might like the smell of it.

It was five miles to the track at the bottom of Hanter Hill but the really hard part came after that where the path got very steep. Once he reached the top Harry stopped to drink some water and looked out over the farms.

In one or two fields there were tractors ploughing wonderfully straight lines and neat curves. In others, trailers and big boxes stood ready for the potato harvest. And over there ... were they sheep? Something was drifting like a cloud towards the corner of a field next to where tiny cows stood almost still, grazing quietly. It *was* a flock of sheep, and something had stampeded them!

Harry jumped to his feet. He thought he could just make out two dots zigzagging behind them but they were too far away to see properly. *You'd need to be a hawk to see exactly what's going on over there*, he thought. And suddenly his hand was slapping at his pocket, feeling for his key-ring.

The little white plastic cards clicked together as he pulled it out. *This really is an emergency*, Harry thought. *I need help from something with better eyesight than mine.* He fanned out the dinosaur cards in the palm of his hand. One of them already glowed and was hot to touch. The creature was greyish but marked with spots of yellowy orange. It had a very sharp beak and something rising from the top of its head like a sail.

Perfect! thought Harry. His heart was pounding fast. 'I know you!' he called, and he swept his thumb across the length of the creature – *nose-to-tail.*

*W*HOOSH!

Chapter 8

The pteranodon appeared without a sound,
resting on its belly on top of Hanter Hill.
Its size made Harry gasp. Its great skinny
wings hung down over the steep slopes,
gripping them as if the hill were an egg
waiting to hatch. Harry had expected to see
something raw and bald, like a bat. Instead
he saw soft red feathers, bright as a parrot's,
along the front edges of the amazingly long
wings.

The creature's head made his heart race,

too. It was like the woodpeckers he had
seen drilling for bugs on the branches of
a dead apple tree in the orchard. Harry
looked nervously at the sharp beak that was
longer than his outstretched arms. Right
now he was hoping not to get mistaken for
a tasty bug himself.

Pteranodon cocked his great head on
one side and the tall triangle of his crest
flashed like red silk with splashes of yellow
in it. Two sets of eyelids, one up, one down,
closed over an eye the size of a cannon-ball.
Was that a wink?

'We meet at last,' said Pteranodon in

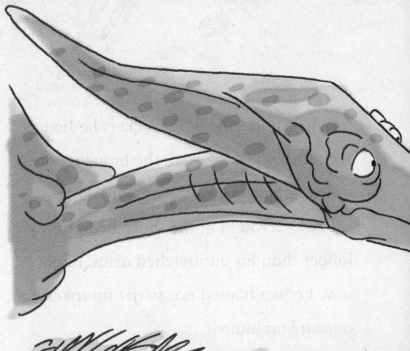

a wheezy voice. 'It's always a pleasure to meet a believer. Do you need me to save someone?'

'N-no,' said Harry. It still shocked him every time to see a B.U.D. up close like this.

'Please don't be scared,' said the winged giant. 'I have quite a large brain and I am at your service. You need to fly, I expect. Fine. I came prepared for that. I am exactly the right size and weight to carry you. We can adjust, you know. Did Spinosaurus tell you?'

'Y-y-y-yes,' said Harry. When
Spinosaurus had awarded him the key-ring,
he had explained that he could make the
dinosaurs as big or as small as he needed
them. But right now he was trying to work
out how he was going to ride this scary
beast. The dinosaur had a cluster of 'fingers'
at the middle edge of each wing. Harry
couldn't see how they could hold him.

'Do you mind if I take a look at your
back feet?' asked Harry.

'Not at all. Shall I show you how I place
them for take-off?'

Harry nodded and Pteranodon made a
little jump, pulled his back legs under him
and squatted down. There were four claws
on each foot – but they weren't quite what

Harry expected to see. He had thought
they might be sharp talons, weapons used
for gripping or tearing, like the ones on
a buzzard or an eagle. In actual fact,
Pteranodon's enormous feet were flat and
spread, rather like the webbed feet of a huge
duck.

'Ah, I see you are wondering how I am
going to carry you,' wheezed the dinosaur.
'I am not going to grab you by the pants,
if that's what you were thinking! There's
a more comfortable way.' He stretched his

neck and lowered it. 'Hop aboard!'

It was just low enough for Harry to be able to jump up and grab it like the branch of a tree. But no sooner were his feet off the ground than the creature raised its head. Harry was left dangling from one arm.

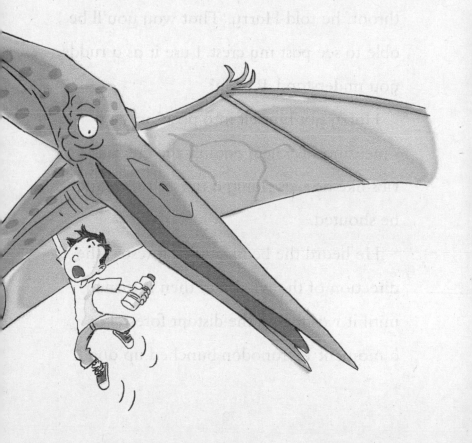

'Hoy!' he shouted and dropped back on to the grass.

'Sorry,' said the dinosaur. He lowered himself to the ground until he rested on his belly like a glider. 'I suggest you lie along my body and hold on tight around my throat,' he told Harry. 'That way you'll be able to see past my crest. I use it as a rudder, you understand. Ready?'

Harry got himself into position, squeezing his knees against the creature's ribs like he was riding a horse. 'I'm ready!' he shouted.

He heard the beast sniff as it tested the direction of the wind and then it turned until it was facing the distant forest. For a moment Pteranodon bunched up and

scuttled forward on his two flat feet, rocking
Harry about in a way that made him
squeal. But a sudden push from the back
legs and over the edge of the hill they went!

Chapter 9

There was hardly any noise at all up in the air, except for a slight rattling from the creature's red crest as it vibrated in the wind. Harry had never been up in a glider plane, but he guessed it might feel like this. The thrill of it!

And then there was the dizzying view, as the fields spun and blurred together below. 'We seem to be going up. Can we go down?' asked Harry to a spot on the back of the reptile's head where he guessed

the ears
might be.
'But . . .
um . . . slowly.'

'Your wish is my command,'
said Pteranodon. 'Hold tight.' He folded
back his wings, tipped forward . . . and
down they plunged.

Wow! was all Harry could think. He
heard someone screaming and realized it
was him. The force of the air rushing at him
blew out his cheeks and made him squeeze
his eyelids together. The fields were coming
towards them at an alarming rate! There
was a whistling in his ears now and Harry
knew for certain that they were about to
crash.

Except they
didn't. Calmly,
Pteranodon stretched out
his wings and they slowed right
down. Harry's tummy took a little while
to catch up with the rest of him, but he was
too excited to worry about that.

'Sheep,' he said aloud suddenly. It was important to remember that he was on a serious mission and not on a ride at the funfair.

'Is this what you wanted to see?' asked Pteranodon politely, skimming over a hedge and sailing over the backs of a flock of panicking woolly ewes. 'Hereford Ryelands, I believe. Yum!'

'They're not for you to eat!' Harry told Pteranodon quickly. He could hear the terrified thunder of the sheeps' hooves and their hopeless *maaaaa!* cries. And there, crazily running in circles around them, were two dogs: one a black-and-white Border collie and the other a small brown terrier.

'Oh no!' shouted Harry, recognizing them both straight away. The collie with

the white ear and eye-patch was Jeff,
who belonged to Mr and Mrs Temple at
Flag Station Farm, down at the bottom
of Harry's village. He was a friendly
dog, always wandering about the village
wagging his tail, chasing bikes and wanting
you to throw sticks for him.

As for the little terrier, he was none other
than Lady Spansford's pet, Spike!

The dogs didn't seem to be trying to
harm the sheep, only round them up.
Unfortunately the farmer pointing his
shotgun didn't see it that way! He was
leaning over the gate from the field where
the cows were grazing, concentrating on
trying to get a clear shot at one of them.

'Get away, Jeff!' yelled the man. So he

knew it was Jeff, too! He'd probably seen him with Mr Temple at the market. 'And you, too, you little beggar!' He aimed the gun at Spike but couldn't shoot because he was too close to the sheep.

Harry thought quickly. Thankfully the farmer couldn't see the flying dinosaur, but Harry wasn't invisible. He had to be careful. 'Fly round behind him,' he instructed. 'You've got to grab that gun before he shoots,' he gasped. 'Leave the rest to me.'

Pteranodon tilted his wings and circled the field, then swooped low over the farmer's head. As he snatched away the gun with his beak, Harry reached down in front of the wing, pushed the man's hat over his eyes and gave him a shove. He staggered

and dropped on to his backside among the
cowpats.

'Quick! Get the dogs away before he
comes to his senses!' Harry ordered.

EEE-OWWWWW! Down they swept

again! Harry looked down the beak of his flying B.U.D. and saw that the collie was right in line to feel the point of it!

Pteranodon let the shotgun drop. He began to mutter and squawk.

'Behave yourself!' warned Harry, which was just enough to save Jeff from getting speared like a sausage. Still, it didn't stop Pteranodon giving the dog's tail a sharp tweak, just for the fun of it.

The dog yelped and shot under the hedge with his wagger tucked firmly between his legs. *Jeff won't go sheep-worrying again in a hurry*, thought Harry.

'Now grab the other dog!' he ordered. 'But no games this time! Just get him by the collar.'

Round they swept once more, and
down so low this time that Pteranodon's
trailing legs slapped against the uncut
hedges. He dipped his head, caught hold of
Spike's collar and flipped him into the air.
Up he went, spinning like a football, and

landed on the dinosaur's wing before rolling

towards its other passenger.

'Gotcha!' said Harry as he grabbed on

to the dog with one hand. 'I think it's time

to take you home to the Manor!' He bent

forward to give new orders to Pteranodon.

'Head east along the valley road but keep out of the way of anybody who might be looking up. I don't want anyone to see me.' He looked back towards the farmer, who was still staggering about looking for his shotgun.

Pteranodon kept low till they could duck behind the next hill where it was safe to start gaining height. As they rose over a field where potatoes had been dug up, Harry saw a chilling sight.

'An accident!' he gasped. 'A tractor's tipped over on its side! Quick! Let's get down.'

Swiftly they landed. Harry, still clutching Lady Spansford's naughty little terrier, slid off Pteranodon's back and dashed towards the tractor. The farm machine had rolled sideways down the steep slope and now the driver lay trapped under the cab.

By his side a dirty brown shape stirred. It leapt to its feet as Harry approached.

'BWOOOF! BWOOOF!'

Chapter 10

'Shaky!' cried Harry, rather nervously it has to be said. He took the damp T-shirt out of his back pocket and held it towards the dog. The smell of Frederick seemed to relax Shaky and Harry patted him on the head carefully. Spike joined in the welcome, wiggling and licking the big dog's anxious face.

'Good boy! Good boy!' said Harry, as something dawned on him. Shaky had run all the way to the Batch not to worry sheep at all – but to find help for his injured master.

'My legs!' came a whisper from the man trapped under the tractor. 'Get this thing off my legs!'

Harry looked at his mobile. No signal.

'Now what?' he said aloud.

'I'm sorry, Harry, but I can't help,' said Pteranodon. 'I haven't got the strength to shift anything as heavy as that. My hollow bones would snap.'

'I understand,' said Harry. 'I'll have to find something stronger to do the job.'

Harry ordered Pteranodon to fly Spike back to the Spansfords' estate and then return with his bike from the top of Hanter Hill. 'Be quick – I'll need you to help me again.'

The dinosaur flapped off with Spike clamped between his two flat feet. The injured farmer was moaning softly. Harry held his water bottle to the man's lips and poured a small amount into his mouth. Then he gave Shaky a drink. The dog lapped gratefully from his hands and then lay back down beside the farmer for comfort.

Harry reached into his pocket and pulled out his B.U.D. key-ring. Two cards on his key-ring were very warm. He swept his thumb across each in the correct direction: *nose-to-tail*. Instantly he found himself almost sandwiched between two mighty bodies as hard as warm brick walls.

Triceratops and Stegosaurus had arrived.

'At your service, Harry,' they rumbled, their voices like low thunder.

Shaky began to stir and look about and growl. Although he couldn't see them, he could smell the dried mud of ancient swamps on the wrinkled hides of the great beasts.

'It's OK,' Harry said, patting him. 'Lie down.' The dog returned to his master, who now looked like he was sleeping.

I have to hurry, Harry thought. *He needs to get to hospital.*

'Can you get your heads under the side of the tractor?' Harry asked his two new super-sized helpers.

Triceratops and Stegosaurus nodded.

They stood on either side of the powerful
machine and lifted it as if it were no
heavier than a dry leaf.

'Now put the tractor over on its other side,' said Harry. He realized that when help did arrive, there might be some very awkward questions. Somebody might like to know how a young boy could lift up a machine weighing over a tonne.

Harry asked the two dinosaurs to stand close to the injured man and help Shaky to keep him comfortable with their warm breath.

He looked into the sky and could see Pteranodon flying low, one leg looped through his bike. *Let's hope nobody is looking up at the sky*, Harry thought, imagining how it would look to see just a bicycle flying through the air. The creature dropped his bike to the ground and landed

beside him with a thump.

'Thank you,' said Harry, patting the side of the beast. But there was no time to waste. 'Do you happen to know Morse code?' he asked.

The creature blinked at him. 'I know about eating fish and flying,' came the answer.

'Never mind. I'll ask Stegosaurus. Would you like to make your loudest call?' said Harry. 'I want you to sound it like this: *Dit-dit-dit, DAH–DAH–DAH, Dit-dit-dit*. And keep it up until I tell you to stop.'

Harry had to cover his ears as an ear-splitting screech blasted out across the fields and the bony plates along the creature's spine rattled. Shaky jumped to his feet and started yapping, adding to the noise. Harry hoped that someone was near enough hear it.

It was certainly loud enough for Dennis Willetts to hear. He was a farmer who was cutting wood at the back of his cottage on the next farm.

He listened again. 'That's an S.O.S.,' he said aloud. He shouted to his wife, who was taking the wood to the shed in a wheelbarrow, 'Mary, can you hear that?'

Mary stopped to listen. 'I can,' she said. 'That's Morse code. Someone must need help.'

They jumped into their Land Rover and
raced up and down the lanes, trying to work
out where the emergency signal was coming
from.

Chapter 11

Back at the tractor, as soon as help had arrived, Harry stroked Triceratops and Stegosaurus in the opposite direction – *tail-to-nose* – to make them disappear. 'You did really well. Great job, both of you!' he said, and he could see how pleased the creatures were as they vanished from his sight.

Right up to the moment when Mr and Mrs Willetts arrived, screaming to a halt in their Land Rover, Stegosaurus had continued to screech his S.O.S. The farmer and his wife jumped out and looked around, wondering where the sound was coming from.

'You can stop now,' Harry commanded the B.U.D. and luckily Mr and Mrs Willetts were too busy worrying about their injured neighbour to hear him.

'It's poor old Ralphie Grimes,' Mary told Harry. 'He must have got crushed by the tractor and somehow crawled out from under it. I saw him ploughing this field yesterday. He lives by himself, so I bet he's been lying here since then,' she said. 'The strange thing is he feels quite warm. Amazing!'

'How did you find him all the way up here?' Mr Willetts asked Harry, as his

wife went back to the house to phone for
an ambulance. 'And what on earth was
making that incredible noise?'

Harry had to think quickly. He explained
that he was cycling about, looking for a lost
dog, when he heard Shaky barking. When

he went to investigate, he found the dog's master lying hurt on the ground and wasn't sure what to do. 'And then, um . . . I looked in the tractor and I suppose an emergency alarm-system must have activated. Lucky you heard it!' he exclaimed.

'Well, Mr Grimes should be fine as soon as the ambulance gets here,' said Mr Willetts. 'The only thing is we need to do something about his dog.' He bent down and stroked him tenderly. 'You deserve a medal, you do, Jakey!'

So that's the dog's real name! thought Harry. Frederick wasn't far off – no wonder he answered to Shaky!

He suddenly realized that Mr Willetts was still talking to him. 'They're bound to keep Mr Grimes in hospital for a couple of days at least,' he was saying.

'Don't worry,' said Harry. 'I know somebody who's going to be *delighted* to look after Jakey for a while.'

Harry stayed long enough to see the air ambulance come and pick up the injured farmer and then he collected his bike from where Pteranodon had delivered it and cycled across the field to the Willetts' farm with the dog trotting along behind him.

Pteranodon flew high above them, circling
around anxiously.

At the farmhouse Mary gave Shaky the
remains of a large chicken they'd shared for
lunch, and a big bowl of water. Her husband
gave the dog a welcome wash-down with
the garden hose, then a good brushing.

Soon Shaky was looking much more his old self and less like a hungry wolf! Harry ate a chicken sandwich and a large glass of orange juice before heading on his way, the dog trotting along by the bike. He'd promised he would bring back Shaky once Mr Grimes was back on his feet.

By now, Pteranodon had settled and was patiently waiting for Harry next to the potato field to see whether he could be of any further service. He explained that when he dropped Spike off at the back door of the Manor, the cheeky little terrier dived into the house through the cat-flap.

'So that's how he sneaks out!' said Harry.

Pteranodon was amazed by the noisy whirling bird that had carried away the injured farmer. 'What a wonderful roar he had!' he said with enthusiasm. 'But what a strange wing-action! He must get very dizzy!'

Harry nodded. He wasn't sure how to explain the helicopter to the ancient

reptile. 'Thanks for all your help,
Pteranodon. You were the real hero.'

'No problem,' replied his personal
aircraft. 'If you need any of us to help you
again,' he wheezed, 'then you know how
to call on us. You don't need Morse code
either!'

Then he shuffled over to Harry so the
boy could stroke him – *tail-to-nose* – and all

of a sudden it was just Harry and Shaky, who was running about and chasing his tail.

'C'mon, boy,' said Harry. 'Someone I know wants to see you!'

Chapter 12

The GOGOs were all starting to worry about Harry when he finally came freewheeling down the hill towards the bakery to meet them. They were planning to shout 'Where have you been?' but they were so surprised to see Shaky trotting behind on a string lead that they all shouted 'Well done!' instead.

Siri, Jack and Charlie crowded around their friend to ask what had happened.

'I was just lucky,' said Harry. 'I was riding

down the lane when I heard Shaky barking. And that's a sound you can't mistake, as you all know.'

All the GOGOs nodded.

He told the rest of the story – well, as much as he could. And it wasn't long before the whole village had heard about it, too, not only about Harry being a hero, but about two dogs from the village getting up to no good.

The way Mr Oakley told it to the GOGOs, a farmer had reported that Jeff the collie had been spotted with a little terrier chasing sheep. 'They were both very lucky not to have got shot,' he reported. Mr and Mrs Temple from Flag Station Farm were very sorry. They realized that Jeff was a working dog and missed his old job, so they bought half a dozen ewes to keep him busy.

Lady Spansford wouldn't hear anything bad said about her little terrier. 'Well, the terrier that worried those sheep simply *can't* have been our Spiky,' she insisted to Mr Oakley. 'We never let him out of our sight!'

'Ask her to check her cat-flap,' Harry suggested to Mr Oakley. 'I mean he might just be able to squeeze through it when she's not looking.'

And when Mr Oakley did mention this to Lady Spansford on the telephone, she said, 'Oh gosh! I see what you mean. I'd never thought of that!' A few minutes later she rang back to beg Mr Oakley not to mention the cat-flap to anyone else. 'And by the way,' she added, 'the Colonel and I would like to offer you – quite free of charge, of course – the use of one of our fields. We feel that your cows would enjoy some fresh grass.'

As for Frederick, he was told that if he was very good and very nice to all the GOGOs, they would lead him to their secret hideout for a wonderful surprise. He enjoyed being blindfolded and led to the Great Oak and he was *overjoyed* to be reunited with his lost friend, Shaky. After

that he was a completely changed little boy. He was happy, well-behaved and everything grown-ups like, except clean, which didn't matter very much.

'Who would have thought that our little boy could become so *sweet* in just three days?' were Mrs Brattburger's words when they got back from Scotland. 'What a family!' Then she covered Harry with wet kisses, and gave his mother lots of extra work writing articles about children and animals. They were even happy to care for Shaky until Mr Grimes was out of hospital and felt able to look after him again.

Best of all, Mr Brattburger presented Harry with a cool battery-powered model of an F-22 Raptor stealth fighter plane.

'I heard about the – um – accident with your model plane,' he said. 'So this is just our way of saying sorry, and thanks for being so good to Frederick.'

Naturally, Harry took it down to the Great Oak and told the GOGOs that it was theirs as much as his.

'Wow,' said Jack. And just in case that wasn't enough, he added, 'Cool!'

'My goodness!' exclaimed Siri. 'It has a two-channel radio and a throttle for 3-D control with independent thrust from separate motors!'

'What? Say that again in English,' said Charlie. 'Oh, never mind; it's great to fly anyway! Don't you think so, Harry?'

'Great to fly?' said Harry, who was daydreaming about something else. 'Oh, yes, it really is!'

It all started with a Scarecrow.

Puffin is seventy years old.

Sounds ancient, doesn't it? But Puffin has never been
so lively. We're always on the lookout for the next big
idea, which is how it began all those years ago.

Penguin Books was a big idea from the mind of
a man called Allen Lane, who in 1935 invented
the quality paperback and changed the world.
**And from great Penguins, great Puffins grew,
changing the face of children's books forever.**

The first four Puffin Picture Books were hatched in 1940 and the
first Puffin story book featured a man with broomstick arms called
Worzel Gummidge. In 1967 Kaye Webb, Puffin Editor, started the
Puffin Club, promising to **'make children into readers'**.
She kept that promise and over 200,000 children became
devoted Puffineers through their quarterly instalments of
Puffin Post, which is now back for a new generation.

Many years from now, we hope you'll look back and
remember Puffin with a smile. **No matter what your age
or what you're into, there's a Puffin for everyone.**
The possibilities are endless, but one thing is for sure:
whether it's a picture book or a paperback, a sticker book
or a hardback, **if it's got that little Puffin
on it – it's bound to be good.**